MYSTERY IN THE OLD RED BARN

Mystery
IN THE
Old Red Barn

By HELEN FULLER ORTON

ILLUSTRATED BY ROBERT DOREMUS

J. B. Lippincott Company
PHILADELPHIA & NEW YORK

*Dedicated with affection
to each boy and girl
who reads this book*

OTHER BOOKS BY HELEN FULLER ORTON

Historical Stories

The Winding River
The Brave Frontier
A Lad of Old Williamsburg
Hoof-Beats of Freedom
The Gold-Laced Coat
The Treasure in the Little Trunk

Fiction for Younger Boys and Girls

Mystery over the Brick Wall
Mystery in the Old Cave
Mystery in the Pirate Oak
Mystery Up the Winding Stair
Mystery Up the Chimney
Mystery of the Lost Letter
Mystery at the Old Place
Mystery of the Secret Drawer
Mystery at the Little Red Schoolhouse
Knights of the Snowstorm
The Secret of the Rosewood Box
Grandmother's Cooky Jar
Danny's Country Store

Farm and Animal Stories

Cloverfield Farm Stories
The Little Lost Pigs
The Little Lost Pigs in Town
Prancing Pat: The Story of a Horse
The Twin Lambs
Queenie: The Story of a Cow

CONTENTS

MYSTERY IN THE OLD RED BARN

I

THE OLD BARN

KATHIE WILLIAMS was standing at the back window of the dining room looking glumly out of doors.

It was a rainy Saturday in October. The maple trees that had been so pretty a week before had now lost most of their leaves.

"There's no fun outdoors today. I'll do my homework first, then read that book I got from the library," she said to Mother, who was making out her grocery list.

"A good idea," Mother agreed.

"Where is Reed?" Kathie asked.

"He went to the village on an errand for me before the storm began. He rode his bicycle, so I suppose he won't come back till it stops raining."

Kathie went upstairs to her room and took out her arithmetic. For half an hour she was busy with pencil and note book, a scowl sometimes on her pretty face.

After a while she sighed and looked out of the window.

"There's a break in the clouds," she said to herself. "Maybe it will stop raining soon."

A moment later she heard Mother calling, "Kathie! Kathie!"

She went to the head of the stairs and said, "Yes, Mother."

"Please come down. I'd like you to do an errand for me."

"All right, Mother."

She put away her arithmetic and notebook, brushed her hair, then ran downstairs.

"What do you want me to do?" she asked.

"I'd like you to go to the old barn and bring up enough apples to make an apple pie."

"Surely. It will be fun to go to the barn on a rainy day, for a lot of birds will be there out of the storm."

She put on her raincoat and her rubber boots. Going to the storeroom she took up a small basket they called the apple basket and was starting off.

"Hadn't you better pull up the hood of your raincoat?" Mother suggested. "You'll get your hair wet."

Kathie had lovely light brown hair, a little curly.

"I don't care if it does get some rain on it," she said. "It will curl more if it's a bit damp."

She did pull up the hood when she reached the back porch because she found it was still raining quite hard.

"Don't stay in the barn to play," said Mother. "I want to have an early lunch today, as I may go to a committee meeting this afternoon if the rain lets up."

Kathie hurried down the steps and followed a well-worn path to the head of the lane that led down to the barn.

The Williams family had been living in the country only two years. Father had bought this small farm then so they could have a pleasant place to live away from the crowded city.

Father didn't do the work on the farm. He had to go every day to his office in the city ten miles away. Sometimes he had to go on a long trip on business for his company. Now he was away in far-off Alaska.

Kathie liked to walk in the rain if it wasn't coming down too hard. She tripped along over the wet grass, down the lane, which was about a quarter of a mile long.

The old red barn stood in the middle of a grassy yard, where little knolls and hollows and a running brook made a wonderful place to play on pleasant days. She and Reed had named it the Barn Meadow. They liked to stop and sail little chips on the brook.

"It's too rainy to stop today," Kathie said to

herself. So she crossed the brook on the little bridge and followed a well-worn path toward the old barn.

Once upon a time the barn had been painted red, but for many years it had not been painted at all, so it had turned gray, with patches and streaks of red here and there.

"It's a long walk to the barn on a rainy day," Kathie was thinking, as she plodded along through the rain. "I wonder why it was put so far from the house."

Then she remembered what she had been told. The house used to stand down here, not far from the barn. A few years ago the owner had the house moved up to the road; but the barn had been left where it had always stood since pioneer times.

Kathie hurried along and soon she came to an incline that led up to the big double doors of the barn.

Up the incline she hurried, unfastened the doors and pulled one of them open far enough so she could go through with her basket.

"It's awful dark in here today," she said to herself, when she had stepped inside.

On each side of the big center floor there was a haymow—a big space in which hay or straw or grain could be put. The mow on the right was filled with sweet-smelling hay reaching far above her head. The one on the left was filled with straw.

Many a good time had she and Reed had on those mows. Sometimes her friend Linda, who lived on the next road to the south, came up the Far Lane; and the three of them had fun playing hide and seek.

"I wish Linda were here now," she said to herself.

She could hear the cooing of doves, away up in the dim shadows under the roof.

"What a pretty sound that is!" she thought. She looked up toward the roof but couldn't see the birds in the dim light.

On a sunny day there would be streaks of sunshine coming through the cracks between the boards that made the walls of the barn, but not today.

Suddenly there was a flutter of wings above her head. "Swallows! The swallows have come in out of the rain," she said, as she gazed upwards and could see them flying under the rafters.

"How many interesting things there are in an old barn!" she said to herself.

Through the tiny windows away up in the gable ends of the barn the birds could fly in and out whenever they chose.

In one corner of the barn floor there was a big pile of apples, put there to stay till cold weather came, when they would be taken to the house and put in the cellar.

Kathie filled the basket with the biggest red apples. "I must hurry to the house," she thought. "Mother will be wanting these."

There was a basement under the whole barn and a narrow stairway leading down to it. And in the basement was the horse stable, where in former times the owner had kept his horses. She had noticed, when she was crossing the meadow, that the outside stable door, where the horses went in and out, was open.

Since Mr. Williams didn't do the farming

himself, but let a farmer on the South Road do it on shares, he had no horses, so the stable was empty.

"I wish there was a horse in the stable," Kathie thought. "I wish we had a nice gentle horse that Reed and I could ride, as we did last summer when we were at Grandpa's farm."

Suddenly she stood stock still, frightened, for there was a sound from downstairs.

"I wonder who's down there," she thought.

When, in a moment, there was another sound, a loud sneeze, and a step on the stairs, she grabbed the basket of apples and dashed through the big front doorway.

Across the Barn Meadow she ran, across the little footbridge over the brook, and on up the lane.

When she reached the head of the lane, Reed was there to meet her, for the rain had stopped and he had come back from the village.

"Why are you running so fast?" he asked.

"There's someone in the old barn. Someone sneezed and I heard the stairs creak!"

"I'll bet you just imagined it. Stairs in old buildings often creak of their own accord."

"I'm sure someone was there," she declared. "You would have run yourself if you had been there all alone and heard those sounds."

"I'll go down and find out," Reed said. He

was twelve and wasn't afraid of anything.

"Wait a minute. I'll go back with you," said Kathie.

She ran in and handed the basket of apples to Mother.

"It won't be long till lunch time," Mother told her. "I'll blow the horn ten minutes before it's ready; and you must come at once."

"We will," Kathie promised, and hurried after Reed.

II

KATHIE'S WISH

As they started out, the rain was only a drizzle. The long wet grass in the lane brushed against their legs; and every once in a while they came to a mud puddle.

They hurried along the narrow path that led to the incline and raced up to the big barn doors. Reed quickly opened one of the doors wide enough for Kathie to go through. Then he pulled it wide open and pushed a stone against it to keep it there.

"It will be nice to have light in the barn," Kathie said.

Reed ran onto the big barn floor and stood in the center of it listening.

"There are no creaks from the stairs now," he said, "but I'll go down to see if there's anybody in the stable."

"Don't go clear down," Kathie urged him.

But Reed was already halfway down the short stairway which led from a little landing. It was

very narrow and steep and was hidden from sight to a person standing on the big barn floor.

Reed stayed down in the basement a few minutes. Kathie waited in fear he would really find something scary.

Finally she went to the head of the stairway and called down, "Reed! Reed!"

After a moment of silence she heard his voice saying, "All right. There's nothing down here but Snooky. And a cat can't make stairs creak."

"Probably whoever it was has gone away, and I'm glad he has."

When Reed came up a moment later, he was followed by a beautiful cat with a tortoise-shell coat, yellow and white, with flecks of brown.

"Did *you* make the stairs creak?" Kathie asked.

But Snooky only arched her back and walked away in a stately manner.

"Let's see how many different sounds we can hear," said Kathie. "Keep quiet as a mouse."

That was a hard thing for Reed to do, but he stopped whistling and stood quiet. They could hear the doves cooing up under the eaves.

"There are a lot of doves in the barn today," Reed said.

"Swallows too," said Kathie.

The swallows didn't stay quietly on the beams close under the roof, as the doves did. Every once in a while one of them seemed to give a signal and they all flew around just under the roof.

"Their wings seem to make a sound like a harness creaking," said Kathie.

"They always sound like that," said Reed. "And I'm sure I hear a cricket in the hay and a squirrel scurrying along a rafter."

"And there's an owl up in that corner, sitting on a beam," said Kathie. "But he's not making any sound, for owls don't hoot in the daytime."

At that moment a weird sound came from

the owl's corner. At first they were startled and a bit scared; then they both laughed.

"Are we going to be afraid of an owl?" Reed asked. "Owls *do* hoot in the daytime once in a while, I guess. Maybe he thinks it's night because it's so dark here."

"An old barn is surely an interesting place," Kathie remarked.

Suddenly Reed put his hand on her shoulder. "You're IT," he said. "Let's play tag."

Quick as a wink he reached the straight ladder that was built against the haymow and climbed up to the top. Kathie threw off her raincoat and was swift on his track.

"That wasn't fair. You didn't give me notice," she accused him, "but I'll catch up with you soon."

She was agile and swift on her feet. Reed ran toward the front of the barn along a broad oaken beam, then across the scaffold that was high above the barn floor to the wide beam on the other side.

Kathie followed carefully at first till she reached the other side of the scaffold, then she hastened her speed. Twice around they went; then she came up with him and tagged him.

"You can't catch me!" she called out, as she started off onto the other scaffold, the one at the back of the barn.

It took three times around before Reed caught up with her and tagged her.

"You surely can run, Kathie," he admitted. "I'll bet there isn't another girl in school who could run on all those high beams and scaffolds and not fall off."

He bowed to her as if she were a queen.

"Aren't we lucky to have this old barn to play in, Reed?"

"I should say so, Kathie."

"Yes, and it was thoughtful of Father to have enough hay and straw put in to fill the mows 'cause it's so much fun to jump into them. Let's play tag some more. You're IT this time," said Kathie, tagging Reed and dodging out of reach.

After the strenuous game of tag Kathie felt like resting, so she sat on one of the mounds of hay. Reed took a running jump from the top of the granary into the haymow and disturbed Snooky, who was lying on the hay taking a nap.

"This is one of the nicest places in the world," said Kathie, after listening to the doves and swallows for a few minutes. "There is just one thing more I'd like."

"What's that?" Reed asked from his perch high up over the hay.

"A horse—a gentle old horse that I could ride. We have a good stable for one and plenty of hay to feed one. Now if I'd only—"

She didn't finish the sentence, for at that moment they heard a loud sound—the blowing of a horn.

"There's the horn. It's lunch time," said Reed.

"We'll have to go," said Kathie ruefully. "We haven't been here very long."

She slid from the mound of hay and went down the ladder on that side, while Reed clambered down the other side.

Just as they were starting out the door, they again heard sounds over toward the little stairway.

"There's someone going quietly down the stairs," said Kathie.

"I'll find out this time who it is," Reed said, as he softly stepped toward the little landing.

"Don't go down the stairs," Kathie pleaded. "There might be an old tramp down there."

But Reed had already gone part way down. Kathie waited impatiently for him to come back. Finally she went to the head of the stairs and called him.

"All right. I'm coming."

He came slowly up the stairs. "Someone had been there, I'm very sure," he said. "I found this at the foot of the stairs."

He showed her a clipping from a paper, an advertisement offering a job. "Maybe some young man was out of luck and was staying here nights till he could get a job."

"We won't mind if he stays in our old barn, if only he is careful not to do any damage," said Kathie.

"Of course not," Reed agreed. "And there was another thing. The bridle that always hangs near the door of the stable had been knocked off the peg where it hung and was on the ground. Someone must have been hurrying past it."

"Oh—h!" Kathie exclaimed.

"But there was no one down there now— unless you count Snooky."

They hurried out of the barn and up the lane. The rain had stopped and the sun was appearing from under a cloud.

III

UNCLE BILL

WHEN they rushed into the house, Kathie exclaimed, "The old red barn was fun today, Mother!"

"And I made a big jump from the top of the granary and nearly landed on Snooky," Reed told her.

"What was Snooky doing in the haymow?" Mother asked.

"I don't know. Maybe chasing mice," said Reed.

"And there was someone downstairs," Kathie added. "I heard the stairs creak."

While their mother took up lunch, they told her all about their adventure in the barn.

They were about to sit down to the table when the doorbell rang; and before anyone could get there to open it, someone came in and a familiar voice shouted, "Hi, everybody!"

"Uncle Bill!" Reed exclaimed.

There stood in the doorway a handsome young

man whom they hadn't seen in a long time.

"Hello, Reed!" said Uncle Bill. "You've grown a lot since I saw you last."

Then he reached over and took Kathie's hand and gave her a kiss.

"How is my niece?" he asked. "But I don't have to ask. She looks like a movie star."

He turned to Mrs. Williams, who was looking happy at seeing her brother. "And how is my sister?" he asked, putting his arm around her and kissing her.

"Just fine; and I'm delighted to see you, Bill. You are just in time for lunch."

She set another place at the table. When they were seated, she said, "I hope you'll stay a month!"

"I'd like to, but I'm going on today. There is a job waiting for me on the west coast. I'm to take a plane in three hours."

Uncle Bill had been living in a city a hundred miles away, so they had not seen him often. He was always welcome, for he was the favorite uncle of Reed and Kathie.

"How's school going this year?" he asked.

"Just fine," was Kathie's reply.

"I like it all right," said Reed. "But I'd rather go west with you than go to school every day."

Uncle Bill looked keenly at Reed as he said, "Young man, you'd better like school. And·

you'd better go every day and do your best at your studies if you want to get a fine chance like this one that came to me."

Mother spoke up, "Uncle Bill didn't get this job by spending all his time having fun. He worked faithfully at his studies in his school days."

"Reed does all right in his studies, I'm sure," said Uncle Bill. "Didn't I hear something about his getting all A's on his report card?"

"That was Kathie," said Reed gallantly.

"But you got a lot of high marks," said Kathie. "And you were first in the running matches several times last year," she went on, standing up for her brother, as she always did.

Uncle Bill was Mother's youngest brother. He was a handsome young man, with light brown hair, a pleasant face and keen gray eyes.

When it was time for dessert, Mother said, "I have a fresh apple pie in the oven, but it is too hot to eat now. We'll have it later."

"That will be fine. I'll be glad to have a piece of fine apple pie. What I'd like to do now is to go down to the old barn. I've had many good times in Grandfather's barn. I may live in a big city and not have a chance to play in a barn for a long time."

"Hurrah!" Reed shouted, remembering the many good times he had had with Uncle Bill in the past.

"Goody!" said Kathie.

The three of them started down the lane together—Reed, Kathie and Uncle Bill.

"That old barn looks pretty good on the outside," said Uncle Bill, as they walked across the Barn Meadow.

"It's nice on the inside too," said Reed.

They hurried on over the grassy ground, up the incline and through the big front doors. When Uncle Bill stood in the middle of the barn floor and looked up into the dim shadows, he asked, "What is that in the corner away up on that high beam?"

"An owl. There is one that stays here daytimes," said Reed.

"Owls sleep in the daytime, maybe you know," said Kathie.

"Of course I know that. Aren't there any doves and swallows or any other birds here? There are usually a lot of them in old barns."

"There were a lot of them here this morning, but they flew out when it stopped raining," Kathie told him.

They stood there several minutes, the three of them, looking up into the rafters and talking about the barn. Then Uncle Bill turned to Reed and asked, "How far can you jump on the hay from the top of the granary?"

"I'll show you," Reed replied. And he was halfway up the ladder before anyone could say Jack Robinson.

Kathie and Uncle Bill stepped over to the far side of the floor, where they could see him when he jumped. Reed went up to the top of the granary, which was higher than the haymow and took a running jump. At the edge of the granary, when he leaped, he went flying over humps of hay and landed on the far side of the second hump.

Uncle Bill clapped his hands. "Fine!" he said.

"That's the best jump you ever took," Kathie called up.

"Very good," Uncle Bill admitted. "But I'll beat you. I'm going to try."

He climbed the ladder and went over to the far side of the mow. He took off his coat and looked around for a place to hang it. He took something out of one of the pockets, then discovered a wooden peg and hung the coat there.

Then he went over to the top of the granary. "Watch and see me jump farther than Reed did," he said to Kathie.

Reed grinned. "I'll watch too."

Uncle Bill was tall and lithe, but he hadn't tried to make a long jump in years. He made a short run, jumped off the edge of the granary

roof and made a flying leap over the first hump of hay.

Down he rolled, down the other side of the hump. Snooky happened to be there. She mewed and ran quickly away to a safe distance, then turned and arched her back and sputtered at him.

"I'm sorry, Snooky," he said, "I don't blame you for scolding, but let's be friends."

What with jumping in the hay and exploring the barn, an hour passed. All at once they heard a sound that startled Uncle Bill. "What was that?" he asked.

"The horn. Mother is calling us to the house," Kathie told him.

"Well, well. It doesn't seem very long since we came, but I suppose we'll have to mind when your mother calls."

"Yes—and quick," Reed said.

They all hurried out of the old barn. They walked swiftly across the Barn Meadow. "I'd like to stop and sail some chips down that brook," said Uncle Bill, "but we mustn't stop now." They walked swiftly up the lane.

"I'm sorry I had to call you," said Mother, "but there was a telephone call from the airport. Your airplane is leaving in an hour."

"I must hurry," said Uncle Bill.

"But not before you eat a piece of my apple pie." Mother was already cutting it.

"Sure I can take time to eat that. Maybe I won't have another chance to eat as good apple pie till I come back here, two years from now."

"And a glass of milk with it," said Mother.

Reed and Kathie joined him. Mrs. Williams got the car out of the garage while they were finishing the snack; and then all four started off to the airport.

"Be sure to write to us when you get there," said Mrs. Williams. "And take good care of yourself."

"I'll try," he promised.

"Good-by, Uncle Bill," said Reed.

"Be sure to come back and see us as soon as you can," said Kathie.

"I will. Don't forget me while I am away."

The steps had been wheeled up to the door of the plane. Uncle Bill climbed in and waved to them from a window.

They watched till all the passengers had gone aboard and the door had been fastened tight and the plane began to move along the runway.

They watched till it was out of sight in the distance. Then they got into the car and turned toward home.

IV

THE LOST WALLET

A FEW DAYS later, when Kathie and Reed were coming home from school, they saw a girl riding horseback on a beautiful little brown horse. Kathie gazed in admiration. "I wish I had a horse to ride," she said.

"Why do you want a horse?" Reed asked. "Haven't we a car that takes us everywhere we want to go?"

"Yes, a car is nice to take us places, but I love to ride horseback. That girl is having a fine time trotting along, trotting along. It's different from an auto. It's more fun."

"It would be fun to ride a horse, but if we get one, I'd like one that is young and can go fast. I'd like to ride like the wind, as they do in the movies," said Reed.

28

"Maybe you'd like that kind, but I'd rather have a nice old horse that would be gentle and never throw me off."

They had come to the driveway and raced to see which one would get into the house first. Reed won, but Kathie wasn't far behind.

"What is the matter with you, children?" asked Mother, who was writing a letter at her desk in the living room. "Aren't you tired enough at the close of school not to go dashing around like wild animals?"

"We're tired of sitting still," Reed replied.

"It makes me feel good to run fast," Kathie told her.

"All right, if it makes you feel good, I won't object. What are you going to do next?"

"I'm going to eat some bread and jam, then I'm going to take a ride on my bicycle," was Reed's reply.

"What will Kathie do if you ride off and there's no one for her to play with?" Mother asked.

"Sis ought to have a bicycle too."

"I don't want a bicycle. I want a horse to ride," Kathie told them for the fourth time, as she took a cooky to eat with her glass of milk.

"Horses are old-fashioned," Mother said, with a twinkle in her eyes.

"I don't care. I just want one."

Chancing to look out of the window, Mother was reminded that she had seen the postman put some letters in their mail box.

"Will you go and get the mail, Kathie? I hope there will be a letter from your Uncle Bill. We haven't heard from him since he flew off."

Kathie tripped out to the road, where the mail box was fastened to the top of a post. She opened the box and took out several pieces of mail.

There were two magazines, several large envelopes containing notices and advertisements; then came a letter. On looking at the upper corner, Kathie saw something that brought a gleam to her eyes. She squealed with delight, "From Uncle Bill to Reed and me!"

Hastily closing the mail box, she ran to the house. "Here's a letter from Uncle Bill!"

Hearing the excitement, Reed came in from the back porch. "What does Uncle Bill say?" he asked.

"The letter is addressed to you and Kathie. You open it," said Mother.

Reed carefully cut it open and drew out a large sheet of paper and Kathie stood listening eagerly as he read it aloud:

"Dear Reed and Kathie:
    I had a wonderful trip across our big country. And a grand country it is, with prairies and cities,

rivers and mountains. I thought of you two
many times as I was flying along. I hope you
are both fine and dandy.

I like it out here and think I'll stay a long
time. Will you two please do something for me?
I left something by mistake in the old barn and
wish you would get it and send it to me. I took
my wallet out of my coat pocket so I wouldn't
lose it in the hay when I made those long jumps.
I'm quite sure I placed it on a narrow beam on
the south side of the barn above the haymow.
Then we came away in such a hurry that I forgot
all about the wallet till I was above the clouds
and a thousand miles on my flight. But it should
still be there.

The wallet itself isn't worth much. I had left my good one in my suitcase at the house. But there is something inside it that is very precious to me. It is a small picture of my mother. I always carry it around with me. Please ask your mother to wrap it safely and send it to me by registered mail.

You and Kathie may have whatever money is in the wallet to buy something your hearts are set on. There may be fifty dollars. I was meaning to give you twenty-five dollars at Christmas. You may keep this money instead.

I hope your mother is well and that you two are having good times.

Uncle Bill"

"Jeepers!" Reed exclaimed. "Uncle Bill is a brick!"

"I hope we can find that wallet," said Kathie, "but it's been five days. Maybe it isn't there any more."

"It is just like my brother to give that money to you children," said Mother. "He has a big heart. You must be sure to find the wallet soon. I'll help you wrap the picture. You can run down to the post office Saturday and mail it to him."

"We'll go right down to the old barn now and find it," Reed said.

They were soon on their way down the lane. "What will we do with all that money?" asked Kathie. "We'll be almost rich."

"I know what I'll do with my share," Reed told her. "I'll get a new bicycle with it. My old one is not much good any more. I'll trade it in toward a new one. Maybe the twenty-five dollars will pay the rest. What will you do with your share?"

"I'll buy a horse. That's what I will do with my share."

"Twenty-five dollars won't buy a horse, even an old horse."

"Maybe Father would give me the rest if I had that much to start with," said Kathie hopefully.

They came to the gate at the end of the lane and climbed over it instead of taking the trouble to open it. As they hurried on over the little brook and across the Barn Meadow, Kathie was thinking, "This big yard would be a nice place for my horse to graze. We could leave the stable door open and let him go in and out whenever he pleased."

In Kathie's mind everything was already working out nicely. She would go riding in the meadow at first, where there was soft grass, so it wouldn't hurt her if she fell off. After a time she would go down the Far Lane and on the quiet road where there were not many cars.

When within a few rods of the barn Reed began to run. "I'll beat you to the barn door!" he cried. And he leaped ahead like a deer.

Kathie, taken off guard, was left behind for a few moments, but she could fly over the ground too and was at the big barn door by the time he had it open.

"I think I know where Uncle Bill left the wallet," she said. "I saw him standing in a certain place just before he went up on the granary before he made that long jump."

Reed was halfway up the ladder by this time and she followed. As she hurried after him, she slipped in the soft hay. Reed heard her cry out, "Oh, dear! I've got some thistles in my arms."

She stopped to get them out, giving Reed time to reach the beam first. It was a little above his head. He reached up and ran his hand along the top of it.

"There's no wallet here," he said. "It's gone if it ever was here."

"It *must* be there. That's where Uncle Bill was standing when he took something out of his pocket and reached up."

She was so busy picking thistles out of her hands and arms that she didn't pay any attention to him for a few minutes. Then she heard him say, "I tell you it isn't here. Come and see for yourself."

In a minute, having picked out the last thistle, she hurried over to Reed. She stood on tiptoe and ran her hand along the beam, which was about six inches wide and was part of the framework of the barn.

"You're right. Where could he have put it, if not here?"

"Let's look on the beams all around the hay-mow," Reed suggested.

They stepped through the springy hay all along that south end of the barn, turned at the corner and felt all along the beam on the west end of the mow, then hurried along the wide beam high above the floor at the inside edge of the haymow, to the east end. When they had felt all along that beam and had come back to the place they started from, Reed said, "That's mighty queer. That wallet is not on any of the beams around this whole mow. What could have become of it?"

"Maybe a bird knocked it off with a wing when it was flying around," Kathie suggested. "Let's pull back the hay at the place where I saw Uncle Bill standing that day. Things can slip down out of sight in a haymow."

They set to work pulling the hay away from the side of the barn, feeling between the tufts of hay, looking for a wallet made of brown leather.

After a few minutes Reed declared, "I'll bet someone has been in the barn and stolen it."

"Then I'll never have my horse," said Kathie sadly.

"And I'll have to keep on using my old bicycle," said Reed.

They were standing there talking when they heard the rustle of wings. "There are more doves coming through that little window up in the peak of the barn," said Kathie. "What pretty creatures they are!"

Some of them swooped down before they flew up to their place up among the rafters. Their wings almost touched the beam where she and Reed had searched.

"I'm sure they must have knocked the wallet off. Let's look some more, farther down among the hay," said Reed.

So they went at it again. They pulled back whole armfuls of hay with the dried clover blossoms still clinging to the stems.

Search as hard as they could for half an hour, they didn't find hide or hair of the wallet with its precious contents.

"We'd better go to the house. Mother will be worried about us," said Reed.

They went down the ladder and started toward the big barn door.

"We'll not tell anyone about the wallet," Kathie suggested.

"Of course not. Someone might come and find it first."

They each picked up a big apple from the pile and munched it as they went up the lane.

V

THE GHOST

MOTHER was still at her desk writing letters when they rushed into the living room.

"We can't find that wallet," Reed shouted. "There isn't any wallet there, not on any beam over the haymow."

"We looked everywhere," Kathie added. "We reached down into the hay and we pulled up armfuls of it. We think maybe—" She stopped because she was out of breath.

"Do you mean that Uncle Bill's wallet with the precious picture in it can't be found where he put it?"

"Uh—huh," Kathie replied, her mouth full of apple.

"That is too bad," Mother said. "He will be so disappointed."

"Maybe the person I heard on the stairs came back and found it," Kathie said.

"I'm terribly sorry if that picture is lost," said Mother. "My brother cherished it very much. He had carried it around for years. Our mother died young, you know, when he was only ten. That was his favorite picture of her."

"We'll go again tomorrow and try very hard to find it," Reed promised.

"I'll write to him and tell him about it," Mother said.

"Could you wait a day or two?" asked Kathie. "We'll keep on hunting for the wallet; and if we find it, he needn't be unhappy thinking it's lost."

"Yes, I'll wait a few days before letting him know."

The next day Kathie was home from school first. It was a foggy day. She practiced on the piano for half an hour, then did a crossword puzzle.

"Why is Reed so late today?" Mother asked.

"I guess he stayed to play basket ball."

"I was going to ask him to go down to the old barn and get some apples, so I could make turnovers for dinner. Would you want to go and get them?"

"Yes, I'll be glad to go."

Basket in hand, she went down the lane, softly singing a song as she swung the basket back and forth. The fog was growing thicker. By the time she reached the gate at the end of

the lane, it was so thick she could hardly see the barn.

She climbed over the gate, hurried over the little bridge and went along the footpath to the big front doors. She pulled the right hand one open, though it was a hard thing for her to do.

As she picked up the apples, she heard the doves cooing. Then came the startling hoot of the owl from his corner close to the roof. It was a weird sound, but Kathie knew it was nothing to be afraid of. Somehow, this time it made her feel shivery.

She hurried to pick up the apples till her basket was more than half full.

"I wish Reed were here," she said to herself.

Going to the big front door, she slipped through and quickly closed it after her. She walked down the incline and along the path toward the gate.

The fog had become thicker, even in the short time she had been in the barn.

When she reached the gate, Kathie turned and looked back. It seemed a bit silly that she had been scared.

In the thick mist the barn was not now in sight. She peered into the mist to see if even the windmill could be seen. That was nearer and was painted in bright colors—white with red trimmings.

But what was that thing walking along at the head of the Far Lane? "What is it? What *can* it be?" thought Kathie.

It was something white. It had suddenly appeared from the other lane—the Far Lane that led to the South Road. It could be seen only dimly in the dense fog.

Whatever it was, it was moving slowly, slowly along without making any sound.

Kathie stood glued to the ground. "It looks like a ghost," was her thought. "It looks almost like the ghost of a horse!"

Kathie couldn't move. She just stood there watching, watching, as the white form moved slowly, slowly through the thick fog toward the barn.

"Oh—Oh, dear! It's going into our stable!" she exclaimed under her breath.

Whatever it was, it went through the open stable door and disappeared.

Kathie took to her heels and ran up the lane, the basket of apples swinging back and forth at her side.

When she came near the head of the lane, she saw Reed coming to meet her.

"Mom sent me to find you," he said. "It is getting dark. You shouldn't have stayed so long, Kathie."

He could see that she was trembling and was out of breath from running fast.

"I'm all right. But, Reed, I saw a ghost in the fog."

"You just imagined it, Kathie. There aren't any such things as ghosts."

"But I saw it, Reed, with my own eyes. It wasn't very plain, because of the dark and the fog. It looked like a white horse—only not quite like one."

"Oh, come, Kathie! It was only the mist, whirling and swirling around. You can imagine anything when the fog does that. Once I thought I saw a ghost. It looked like a tall lady dressed in white. I was scared—mighty scared. But when I went nearer, it turned out to be a bush with mist swirling around it. You ought not to let your imagination do such things to you, Kathie. You ought to be more sensible."

"I did truly see a ghost," she declared. "So there! I guess I know what I see."

"In the morning I'll go down to the barn with you and find out about it."

They went quickly to the house. As soon as she stepped into the kitchen, Kathie said, "Oh, Mother, I saw a ghost. It was in the fog!"

"What's that? A ghost?"

"Kathie is silly tonight," Reed told her. "It was just fog."

"Did you see it too, Reed?" Mother asked. "Tell me what it really was."

"No, I didn't see it. I didn't go down the lane, for I met Kathie at the head of it. Of course, she just imagined it."

"That could be, when there is a thick fog," said Mother. "When I was about your age, Kathie, we often saw the mist in the valley. We would stand, my sister and I, at the edge of our garden and look down into the valley where the mist was forming strange shapes. We would talk about them and guess what they looked like. It was interesting and a good deal of fun but they always disappeared when the sun came out."

"But I'm sure," Kathie persisted. "I saw it with my own eyes."

"We'll go down to the barn in the morning," Mother told them.

Saturday morning the fog had cleared and it was a bright sunny day. After breakfast, Kathie said, "Now let's go down to the old barn to find out about my ghost."

"If it *was* a ghost, it won't be there," Reed told her. "They always disappear by morning."

"Anyway, I want to go and find out."

"All right, all right," Reed said.

Mother said it was such a sunny day that she didn't need to go after all; and she had so much to do that she ought to stay at the house and do it.

"Don't stay down there very long," she said. "I'll want to know soon what you find out."

When they came to the gate, Kathie pointed to the head of the Far Lane.

"It was near that place that I saw the ghost first. It seemed to be coming this way in the fog. It went slowly, slowly along and seemed to be tired. It turned toward the barn, but slowly, slowly."

"Anyway, we'll soon find out," said Reed. "Come on."

They walked swiftly along the path toward the open door of the stable, which had been vacant for at least two years. They came to the door, Reed ahead.

"There's certainly no ghost here!" he exclaimed.

Kathie looked relieved but a little disappointed too.

"But I saw one come here," she declared.

"How could you expect a ghost would still be here?"

Kathie only sighed.

"Let's go upstairs and hunt for the wallet again," said Reed.

They climbed the little stairway that led to the big barn floor.

VI

THE WHITE HORSE

"I'LL BE up there first," said Reed. He
darted over to the ladder that was built straight
up against the haymow, reached up and grasped
a rung of it and pulled himself up. He quickly
climbed up and was already hunting for the
wallet when Kathie appeared at the top.

"No doves in the barn this morning," said
Reed. "They have all flown out to enjoy the
sunshine."

"The swallows too," said Kathie, looking up
among the rafters. "But there's the old owl in
its corner."

The place where Kathie had seen Uncle Bill
standing, when he put something on a beam,
was where Reed was now standing, near the
edge of the granary. When anyone was putting
hay down to feed the horses, he pitched it down

to the hayracks from that spot.

"What is the use of searching there any more?" she asked. "Didn't we look there the other day?"

"Maybe we didn't look in every bit of the hay."

As he kept pushing and pulling the bunches of hay, Kathie helped at first, then she sat down on a mound of hay and pulled up stems of clover, to see how many blossoms she could find.

Very quiet she was sitting, listening to all sorts of sounds.

"What do you hear?" Reed asked, after a little, noticing an intent look on her face.

"I hear sounds— Something stepping around down in the stable."

"Oh, Kathie! Imagining things again! Weren't we just down there? Was there anyone there then?"

"No, but I'm sure there is now."

"All right, I'll go down, just to prove to you that there is nothing there."

"I'm going too."

At the foot of the little stairway, Kathie had to walk about ten feet before coming to the door of the stable that opened into the main part of the basement.

Reed was at the door first. Kathie heard him

exclaim, "Snakes and bumblebees! I'll be jiggered!"

"What's the matter?" Kathie asked, as she stepped down to the last step. In the dim light she made a misstep and fell down on the clean straw that covered the basement floor.

"Come, Kathie! Come quick and see what's here!" Reed called.

She got up quickly and hurried over. "Oh!" she exclaimed. "A horse! A white horse! So that was my ghost!"

"Yes," Reed acknowledged. "It must have

been a horse that you saw in the fog."

"A nice old white horse," Kathie murmured softly, as if she were afraid the creature would melt away if she spoke very loud.

"But where did it come from? And how did it happen to come here?" Reed spoke as if *he* were afraid it would melt away if he spoke loudly.

Kathie was looking starry-eyed at the animal standing there so quietly and, it seemed to her, so happily.

She went closer and put out a hand and tenderly stroked the creature's neck.

"I want to be sure it's real," she said.

"It's real, all right," Reed assured her.

"And it's a gentle horse," Kathie said. "See! It lets me stroke its neck without trying to pull away. Do you remember how Grandpa's horse Thunderbolt pulled away and kicked if we went near?"

"Do I remember? I never tried to go very near but once. But you'd better be careful. Maybe this one will kick if you bother it too much."

"Not this horse. I'm sure this is a gentle one." But she drew back a little.

"What I keep wondering is, where did this horse come from? Where was he when we were here before?"

He soon spied something that gave a clue.

The horse had a long thick tail. Reed pulled from it a twig of blackberry bush.

"I know where he was just now. Do you remember that patch of blackberry bushes around on the north side of the barn? He was there, out of sight from us when we came. That is the only blackberry patch in all the Barn Meadow."

"Of course," said Kathie. "Do you s'pose he heard our voices and came to the stable because we were here?"

"What I'm wondering is, why did he come here? And where does he belong?"

"Do you s'pose we can keep him? Do you s'pose I will ever ride him?"

"Probably the owner will show up soon," Reed told her.

Kathie was very quiet for a few minutes, as she looked the horse over from head to foot. "I'm sure this horse is the ghost I saw last night in the fog. It seemed a little bigger though."

"That was because of the fog. Things often seem larger in fog or mist."

Again Kathie patted the horse's neck and said, "Nice horsie! What is your name? Who is your owner?"

"My guess is that he came from a long way off," said Reed.

"Yes, he seems tired."

They were standing there talking, when the horse turned around and went out of the stable and put its head down in the watering trough that stood beside the stable door.

"He's thirsty and there's no water in the trough," Kathie said.

It was a large wooden trough that had been hollowed out of a huge tree. "That horse knows that there is sometimes water in that trough," Reed said. "I believe he *has* been here before."

"He surely has. Can we put some water in? He must be thirsty."

Reed was already running over toward the windmill that stood a few rods away in the Barn Meadow. "I think I can turn the valve in the pipe. If I can, the water will flow down from that tank beside the windmill into the watering trough."

"Oh, Reed, that would be grand."

It was some time since the valve had been turned and it wouldn't budge at first. "I'll have to have a wrench," said Reed. "You wait here while I go up to the barn and get one. I saw one there not long ago."

While Kathie was waiting, she watched the horse walking around and nibbling the grass. "You were hungry and thirsty," she said. "And you look as if your coat hadn't been brushed or curried lately. Were you a long time coming here? And where did you live?"

But the old white horse only moved around slowly and nibbled grass.

Soon Reed came running with a wrench in his hand. "I can turn it with this," he said.

This time with a strong pull with the wrench, the valve began to turn. "Run to the watering trough, Kathie," Reed said. "If the water begins to flow into it, let me know."

She sped over the ground like a deer and stood looking down into the old watering trough. In a few minutes a stream of silvery water began to flow into it. She called, "The water is flowing. It's filling the trough."

How the horse knew, neither of them could say, but soon he came around the corner of the barn and went straight to the watering trough. He put his mouth down in it and began to drink.

Reed came to see how fast it was flowing. "That's grand," he said. "There'll soon be enough for all he can drink."

"He was surely very thirsty," said Kathie. "That shows that he came a long way without finding any water to drink."

"Maybe someone around here will know who he belongs to," said Reed.

"I hope not! Oh, I hope not," Kathie exclaimed.

"Whether he belongs around here or came

from far away, we'll have to give him up sometime," Reed told her.

"Reed," Kathy cried, "we must get some hay down for him." So Reed went up to the loft and brought out some of the freshest hay. But the horse ate only a little.

"Do you s'pose we can ride him?" Kathie asked.

"He seems gentle enough. Suppose I try first."

Reed stepped up on the edge of the watering trough and swung to the horse's back. As if he knew what was expected, the horse started slowly off into the Meadow.

There was no bridle on him, so Reed couldn't guide him, but the gentle old horse walked slowly and carefully over the grassy ground, out of sight behind the barn, then back to the stable door.

Kathie had followed part of the way. "I want to ride," she said, when they returned.

"I must put a bridle on him first," Reed said.

He slid down from the horse's back and went into the stable, where there was a bridle hanging on a peg.

"Do you know how to put it on?" Kathie asked.

"Sure. I learned at Grandpa's last summer."

It wasn't easy, for he must make the horse open its mouth so he could put the bit in, but

he did succeed. Then he fastened the straps.

Once more he climbed up on the horse's back from the edge of the watering trough. "If you want to ride, climb up behind me, Kathie," he said.

She stepped on the edge of the trough and, with some help from Reed, swung up onto the horse's back. They started off around the Barn Meadow.

"Oh, this is grand!" Kathie said, after a bit, when she was no longer afraid of slipping off.

Around the Meadow twice and partly down the Far Lane they rode. There's no knowing how far they would have gone, but soon there came the sound of a horn.

"Mother wants us to come to the house," said Kathie.

Reed turned the horse around and they went back to the barn.

"That was great fun," said Kathie, after she slid down to the ground.

When Reed took off the bridle the horse went directly to the watering trough for another drink. Reed and Kathie ran to the gate and were soon at the head of the lane.

Mother was on the back porch to welcome them. "Oh, Mother, it was a real horse, a live horse," Kathie shouted. "It was a real white horse, not too little and not too big."

"Do you mean that you found a white horse at the barn?"

"We surely did," Reed replied.

"A nice gentle old horse," said Kathie, "and I thought it was a ghost!"

"Well, well! But of course it belongs to someone—who will come for it sometime," said Mother.

"It must have come a long way, for it was very tired," Kathie told her. "But it gave us a fine ride."

"Do you mean that you have already gone horseback riding?" Mother asked in alarm.

"Yes."

"What won't you children do next?" Mother asked. "It might have turned out to be a skittish horse and thrown you off."

"But it wouldn't. It isn't that kind," Kathie assured her.

"I'll go down after lunch and see for myself," Mother told them.

VII

ON HORSEBACK

LUNCH over, Kathie said, "Let's go down to the barn and take another horseback ride, Reed."

"All right, I'm ready."

"Will you go, Mother, and see our horse?" Kathie asked.

"Perhaps; but I may have to go to a committee meeting. I'll go with you unless I get a telephone call."

"I want to polish my bike first, so it will be shiny the next time I ride into the village," Reed said.

Kathie was not allowed to have a bicycle, for there was too much traffic on the road. She took down a favorite book from the book shelves and sat there reading till Reed looked in and called out, "I'm ready, Kathie! Come on."

Just then the telephone rang. Mother answered it. When she rang off, she said, "I have to go to the committee meeting, but if you two will hurry, I'll go down to see that horse first."

So the three of them were soon walking down the lane together. It was a sunny day in late October. Little white clouds floated lazily in the blue sky. The smell of burning leaves was in the air.

"I like fall," Kathie said, as she walked sedately beside Mother. "Sometimes I think it is the best time of year."

"It's a nice season of the year," Mother agreed. "I suppose it seems all the nicer because we know the cold bleak winter will soon be here."

When they came to the gate, Kathie said excitedly, "Look, Mother! There is the horse, over by the windmill."

"Why, it's a fine-looking horse," said Mother. "It's not a horse for drawing heavy loads, I can see that, but for doing light work or drawing a carriage or—"

"For horseback riding," Kathie broke in.

Reed opened the gate for Mother, then he ran over toward the barn and brought back a bridle.

Mother went up to the horse and stroked its neck and spoke gently, "You are a nice horsie! Where did you come from? How did you happen to come here?"

The old horse turned its head to look at Mother, then reached down to nibble grass.

"I won't need to be anxious about you chil-

dren," Mother said. "Let me see you ride the horse a little, then I must go back."

Reed put the bridle on, then climbed up on a stump that was near by. From there he swung to the horse's back.

"Get up," he said. And the horse began to walk slowly off around the Barn Meadow.

Reed sat up straight and urged the horse on; and the first thing they knew, the horse was trotting along and Reed was bouncing up and down, up and down.

When they came back, Kathie said, "I want to ride. I rode last summer at Grandpa's."

"Very well. You may try," Mother agreed.

Reed helped her up. She took hold of the bridle rein. Proudly the horse walked off over the green grass of the meadow, as if he were carrying a queen.

Mother's eyes anxiously followed them. And when Kathie came back triumphantly, Mother said, "I see that you can both ride safely. I don't suppose we can keep the horse long, because the owner will come for him. But meanwhile you will have pleasure taking rides here in the meadow. You may ride in either of the lanes also, but don't go out in the road, where the traffic is heavy. Promise me?"

"Sure," said Reed.

"Of course," said Kathie.

"Now I'll go back to the house and be off to my meeting," Mother said.

She went to the gate and up the lane. And she was thinking, as she hurried along, "They're good children. I wish we could keep that horse for them."

Kathie gazed in admiration as Reed rode over the knolls and along the paths of the meadow.

"Let me ride again," she said, when he came back.

"Climb up behind me," said her brother. He drew up to the old stump and helped Kathie climb to the horse's back.

"This is grand," Kathie said, when they came back to the windmill for the third time.

"This horse is surely a good one for riding," said Reed.

"I do hope we can keep him," said Kathie wistfully. "Do you s'pose we'll ever have to give him up?"

"How can I tell? Let's hope."

After school, every day for the next week they rode the horse around the Barn Meadow and up and down both lanes. Every day they searched in the barn for Uncle Bill's wallet.

One day Kathie heard a call from the Far Lane, "Hello, Kathie!"

There stood Kathie's chum. "Hello, Linda! Come over and see our horse," Kathie called back.

Linda's light curls blew in the wind as she ran up to the windmill, where Kathie and Reed had just dismounted from the horse's back after a fine ride.

"I haven't seen you in ages," Kathie said. "Not for a month, I guess."

"We stayed away on our trip longer than we planned to. We just got back last evening."

"I've missed you," said Kathie. "I'm glad you are back."

Linda was looking with all her eyes at the white horse. "Where did you get that horse?" she asked in astonishment.

"He came here all by himself. He came in a dense fog."

"He looks just like the one that used to live here before you came. He belonged to the man who sold the place to you. I'm sure it is the same one, though he looks much older than when they went away."

Linda went over to the horse and looked him over. "Here are welts on his side," she said. "It looks to me as if someone had struck him with a whip."

"Oh, dear!" Kathie said, with indignation in her voice. "Who would do that to such a nice gentle horse?"

"That is what makes me wonder, for the man who lived here was always kind to his horses. How did you say he came?"

"He just appeared out of the fog. I thought it was a ghost horse when I first saw him. Where did the man go when he moved away from here?"

"I don't know. We were told that it was about thirty miles away."

"Would a horse come back as far as that?" Reed asked. "We have lived in a city and don't know much about horses."

"I suppose a smart horse might."

"Maybe you know his name," Kathie said. "We haven't known what to call him."

"Oh, yes. If he is the same one, his name is

Tom. He was sometimes called Old Tom. I was sorry when he went away, for I was sometimes allowed to ride him."

"I s'pose we'll have to give him up," said Reed. "But we can't unless the owner comes for him, for we don't know where he lives."

Kathie went over to the horse and asked, "Is your name Tom?"

To their great surprise, the horse turned his head and seemed to nod.

"Well, of all things. That must be his name and he knows it," said Linda.

Soon Tom started toward the barn and went to the watering trough. He took a long drink of water before going into the stable.

"If we could only find that wallet, maybe we could buy Tom, if ever the man comes for him," said Kathie.

"What wallet?" Linda asked. "Did someone lose one around here?"

"Yes, in the haymow. Our Uncle Bill left it there and we can't find it."

"I'll help," Linda offered, "but first I'd like a ride on Old Tom. Could I?"

"Sure you may ride him. I'll bring him back here."

"Couldn't all three of us ride him at one time?" Linda asked.

"Maybe." Reed led Tom over to the stump and mounted him.

"Get up on the stump, girls," he said. "I'll help you to mount from there."

In a few moments all three were gaily riding on Old Tom's back. Three times around the Barn Meadow they rode.

"This is the best luck," said Kathie. "I was wanting to go horseback riding; and then this horse came to me through the fog."

Old Tom was evidently through giving rides for the present, for he went to the barn, took a drink from the watering trough and then went into the stable.

"I'll go over and put some hay down into his rack for him to eat," Reed said. "Maybe he is hungry." He went to the stable door.

The girls went through the big front doors. Each of them picked up an apple and they sat on the haymow to eat them as they visited. Linda told about her trip and Kathie had to tell Linda all about what had happened in school during the last month.

VIII

AUNT JANE

REED came up stairs and climbed the ladder. The girls could hear him pitching hay down into the hayrack in front of Old Tom. They could hear the horse stepping around, and then all was quiet down in the stable as Tom pulled the hay down between the spindles of the hayrack.

When Reed had pitched enough hay, he again searched for the lost wallet. They could hear the crackling sounds of the dry hay as he pulled up bunches of it and threw it over to one side.

"What is Reed doing?" Linda asked.

"Hunting for the wallet that got lost in the haymow."

Kathie told her more about Uncle Bill and the lost wallet. "And there was something in it that was very precious to him," she said. "He asked us to find it for him."

"A brown wallet wouldn't be too easy to see if it dropped into the hay," Linda said. "I'll help find it if you want me to."

"Thank you, Linda. He's our nicest uncle, so Reed and I would like to find it for him."

"Let's go up there and hunt for it right now," said Linda.

The two girls climbed the ladder and were soon reaching down into the dry hay here and there.

"I'll find it first," said Linda, pushing her arm down as far as she could reach. "My mother says I'm good at finding things."

"Here it is!" she exclaimed after a few minutes. "I've found the wallet."

Reed came hurrying over. Linda was holding up something that in the dim light looked a bit like a leather wallet. She handed it to Reed.

"That isn't a wallet. That is only an old brown glove."

"Now that I see it plainly, I can see that it isn't a wallet," Linda admitted. "But how did a glove come up in this haymow?"

Kathie spoke up. "Maybe someone was walking in the clover field and dropped her glove."

"Or maybe a dog carried it there," said Reed. "Better luck next time, Linda."

The girls worked harder than ever, each determined to be the first to find it. They pulled handfuls of hay and pushed their hands far down, no matter if thistles did prick them.

After a bit they were startled by a loud "Too—whoo!"

"Where is that owl?" Linda asked.

Kathie pointed to the solemn bird on its perch in the corner. "It certainly gave me a scare," Linda said.

She had to leave before long. "Come again," Kathie invited her.

"Thank you. I'd love to." She went down the ladder and was gone.

For a little while Reed and Kathie kept on hunting for the wallet that meant so much to them and to Uncle Bill.

It wasn't very long before they heard footsteps on the big barn floor. A girl's voice called up, "Hi!"

It was Linda; and her father was with her.

"Good morning, Mr. Whiting," Kathie greeted him.

"Good morning!" he said in return. "I've come to ask a favor. Linda tells me that Old Tom is back."

"Yes, that's so," Reed told him.

"I'd like to hire Tom for a few hours to plough my garden. The man who sold the place to your father used to let me take him every fall for that purpose. I like my garden land to be ploughed in the fall. I used to pay him five dollars for Tom for one afternoon. I'll pay the same to you."

Reed was perplexed. Ought he to let the horse be taken away for that purpose? What if the owner came for him while he was gone?

"My father is kind to horses," Linda said. "He wouldn't use a whip."

"Of course not," said Mr. Whiting. "And one doesn't need to with Tom. He is a faithful horse and does his work well."

"We wouldn't let a stranger have him for any kind of work," Kathie replied; "but we know you wouldn't work him too hard, Mr. Whiting, and you wouldn't be cruel to him. I think we might let you have Tom, but we'd better ask Mother."

"We'll go up to the house and ask her," Reed told Mr. Whiting.

"Very well. You may telephone the answer. If I can have him, I'll do it this afternoon."

Linda smiled to thank them and she and her father left.

Reed and Kathie were about to go down to the stable to see if Tom was still there, when there came the sound of the horn.

"Mother wants us," Kathie said. "Let's go right up to the house." When they reached there, Mother was talking on the phone. "Can

you come and stay with Reed and Kathie for three or four weeks?" she was saying.

They couldn't hear the answer, but evidently the person at the other end had not consented at once.

Mother went on, "I have to go to Alaska. I've just had word that Theodore has had an accident and is in a hospital there. I ought to go at once."

Kathie stood in fear and trembling wondering what had happened to Father.

"That will be fine," Mother was soon saying. "I'd like to go at ten o'clock tomorrow. Can you be here by that time?"

The answer must have been Yes, for she said "Thank you" and rang off.

"Is Father badly hurt?" Reed asked.

"We don't know yet. I hope not. I was talking with Aunt Jane. She will come and stay with you while I am gone."

Kathie's face showed disappointment. Reed's didn't look any too pleased. She wasn't their favorite aunt.

"It is the best I can do for you," Mother told them. "Aunt Jane will cook good meals for you and look after the house nicely. She will take care of you if you should be sick. I'm sure you'll help all you can by making the best of things, won't you?"

"Of course," Reed promised.

"I'll try," said Kathie.

They helped Mother pack her suitcase. They ran errands for her. Each wrote a letter for her to take to Father.

Aunt Jane arrived about dusk. "I hope you have impressed on the children that they are to obey me without any question," she said to Mother.

"Yes, and I'm sure they will try to be helpful and do everything right."

Early the next morning, they all went with Mother to the airport. Aunt Jane was a careful driver and they enjoyed the ride.

As they stood waiting for the signal for her to go on board, Mother said, "I'll come back as soon as Father is better. I don't like to leave you so long, but I must go there and see that he has good care."

Soon the steps were wheeled up to the door of the plane and the announcement went forth over the loud speaker: "Flight 35, to Nome, Alaska. Passengers please board."

Mother said, "I'll be thinking of you every hour."

"And we'll be thinking of you and Father," said Kathie.

"We sure will," said Reed.

"Don't do anything rash while I'm gone, like buying a white elephant," Mother continued, with a smile.

That amused Kathie. She looked up into Mother's face and smiled back, "Buy a white elephant! Of course not. We wouldn't know what to do with one."

Mother went up the steps and through the door of the airplane. They stayed to see the plane go down the runway and fly up into the sky. They stayed till it disappeared in some fleecy clouds.

Then they got into the car and were very quiet while Aunt Jane drove home.

IX

THE STRANGER

MOTHER mailed a letter home from every stop. And after she reached Alaska, she mailed one every day, by air mail.

"It's grand to fly over mountains and prairies and rivers," she wrote. "It's wonderful to fly above the clouds, as we did part of the time."

When she arrived in Alaska, she wrote to Reed and Kathie within an hour. "You'll be glad to know that Father is doing well. His broken leg is in a cast and he will not be able to use it for at least six weeks. I'm glad I came, for it was very boring to him to lie in a hospital alone day after day. I'll take books and magazines to him. We'll play games— chess and checkers and other games of that sort.

"I hope you are both well and that things are going nicely at home. With much love to you both,

Mother."

"That is good news," said Kathie.

"Yes, and I'm glad we could let her go. But six weeks is a long time."

One day Reed forgot to clean his shoes on the mat outside the door before he went into the living room. A harsh voice instantly called, "Reed Williams, never again come into the house, while I am in charge, without making sure you are not going to track in mud."

It was the tone more than the words that made him wince. He wasn't used to hearing harsh tones of voice. If Mother had said the same words in her gentle voice, he would instantly have been sorry.

Most of the time Kathie tried her very best to please Aunt Jane, but sometimes she forgot. One day she came running in from school and turned on the radio for a favorite program. She turned it on rather loud, thinking Aunt Jane might be glad to hear it too.

In a moment the harsh voice came from upstairs, "Don't you know, Kathie, that I always want a quiet hour for a nap at this time of day?"

"I'm sorry, Auntie. I forgot."

"Children shouldn't forget," was the quick response.

In her heart Kathie determined, "I'll really

try to remember the things Aunt Jane doesn't like. I'll try to remember what not to do, even if it isn't easy."

The days were getting shorter, for it was late October by this time. They were getting colder too.

Many a day Kathie and Reed went down to the old barn soon after school and spent some time in hunting for the lost wallet.

Reed wrote Uncle Bill, telling him how sorry he and Kathie were that they hadn't been able to find it. Every day, after looking in some new place for the wallet, Reed put the bridle on Tom and they went horseback riding.

"If it weren't for Old Tom I don't think I could stand it with Father and Mother away so long," said Kathie one day, as she and Reed were riding up the lane.

"I'm mighty glad we can have these good times with Tom," Reed agreed.

"Let's go clear up to the house and let Aunt Jane see how well we can ride," Kathie suggested.

"That's a fine idea," said Reed.

Tom seemed to enjoy it as much as they did. He arched his neck and lifted his feet high as they came near the window where Aunt Jane was reading a magazine.

Kathie let go of Reed and pulled herself up

straight. He held the rein a little tighter and held his head a little higher, to show that he was a good rider.

Suddenly, just as they were passing the window, they heard an outcry. The window was pushed up and Aunt Jane said, "Oh, Kathie, get down from that horse's back at once. And please don't ride him again while you are in my charge."

Kathie couldn't believe her ears. The very thing she most wanted to do—the very thing that gave her great enjoyment these days.

"Oh, please, Aunt Jane! I love to ride horseback."

"I mean Reed too," Aunt Jane said. "It's dangerous to ride a horse you don't know well. You might slide off and get hurt under the horse's feet."

"But I won't, for I hang on to Reed. See."

She put her arms around his shoulders and hung on tight. "Tom never goes fast when we are on his back."

"Horses sometimes get scared at some strange thing that comes along suddenly. Anyway, will you please not ride horseback while I am in charge?"

"Tom isn't strange," Reed told her. "We've ridden him many times and talked to him so much that he knows us."

"He likes us," Kathie added.

Then Aunt Jane went out to the place where Tom was standing, with the two of them on his back. She stroked his neck and patted his back. Tom turned his head and looked at her with his soft beautiful eyes.

She smiled. "I see that he is a gentle horse," she said. "I used to have one nearly like him— a white horse that seemed to like to have me ride on his back. But don't go out on the main road where there are so many cars. Keep to the lanes and the Barn Meadow."

"We will," they promised together.

"We'll ride him back to the meadow and then not ride any more today," said Reed. "Mother said we could ride. And we'll not go on the busy road."

Kathie mounted again, and they rode happily back to the barn. Kathie took out her handkerchief and wiped off the tears that had come when she thought they could ride no more while Aunt Jane was there.

When they came to the end of the lane, Reed slid off the horse, opened the gate and they passed through. He climbed up again and rode over toward the stable door.

Kathie had slid off when they came to the brook and was putting little chips in the water and watching them float downstream.

Shortly she heard someone talking to Reed.

A stern voice was saying, "Why are you riding my horse? I came to take that horse home. What right have you to ride him?"

Reed stopped Tom and looked down at the man. "The horse came to our barn and we like him. We didn't know who he belonged to. We've been taking care of him and riding him."

"I see."

"Who are you, sir? And where do you live?"

"I don't know that it matters what my name is, but it happens to be Steven Plunkett."

"Where do you live, Mr. Plunkett? Near here?"

"Not so very near—about thirty miles away. I mistrusted that Tom had come back here."

On hearing the voices, Kathie left the brook and came over. She stood near by, with a dreadful fear in her heart.

"Must we really give Tom up?" she was thinking. "Must we let him go away when we like him so much and have such good times with him?" She stood there in deep trouble.

The stranger was saying, "I bought that horse from the man who used to live here. His name was Trent. He must have sold this place to you folks."

"That's right. Father bought the farm from a Mr. Trent, who moved away from here, a long way off."

"Yes, and after a year he sold this horse to me. He left home one day about two weeks ago and I wasn't able to find him—till now. I want him back. He's an old horse, to be sure, but he could still draw a milk wagon around."

"I think he's a smart horse to come back thirty miles to his old home," Reed said.

A question came into Kathie's mind. "What was your horse's name? He may not be the same one, just because he's a white horse."

"His name is Tom."

"I guess he's your horse then," Reed said.

"He answered to that name. Will you sell him? My sister and I would like to keep him."

The man considered for a moment. "I might sell him if I got a good price."

"What would be a good price?" Kathie asked timidly.

"I wouldn't part with that horse for less than three hundred dollars," the man said. "And I would want it quick—within three days. That is when I'm going back home."

"Oh, dear! We could never pay that much," said Kathie. "Wouldn't you take less?"

"No. That's my price."

"This horse is old and not very good for work," she told him. "But he's just wonderful for taking us horseback riding. We'd love to have him, but we haven't that much money now; and our folks are far away and won't be back for many more days than three."

"I'll give you four days. I can visit relatives in town. I'll even let you have him for two hundred dollars if you'll have the cash ready then. I'll be here at two o'clock in the afternoon, four days from now. Be sure to keep the horse here all safe."

"He'll be all safe," Reed told the man. "And if we can find the—"

Kathie touched his arm and shook her head.

The man started off toward the main road. "I'm going to catch a bus and go into town for four days," he said. "I'll be back on time. That will be next Saturday."

When he was out of hearing, Kathie said, "It wouldn't be best to let him know about the wallet. He might search and find it."

"You're right, Kathie. Somehow I don't trust that man. I don't think he would treat Tom right if he had him again. I'll bet he swung the whip that made that welt on Old Tom's back."

"Oh, Reed, we must somehow manage to buy Tom and keep him."

"Of course we must," Reed agreed. "We must keep him out of the hands of someone who would be cruel to him. We must manage to get the two hundred dollars somehow."

"And only four days," Kathie murmured. "And Father and Mother far away in Alaska. If only we could find the wallet, that would bring us part of the money."

X

THE SEARCH

KATHIE went up to Tom and patted his neck and told him, "Don't you worry, Tom. Reed and I will keep you here somehow. You won't have to go back to that man who doesn't treat you well."

It seemed as if Tom understood, for he turned his head and looked kindly at Kathie out of his beautiful eyes. Then he went back to the stable.

"Now we must find that wallet, even if the skies fall," said Reed. "We'll search every inch of this old barn to find it."

By this time he was as eager as Kathie to keep the gentle old horse. They both hurried to the barn, climbed to the top of the straw in the north mow and began to pull it up in armfuls and dig deep down into it.

"Uncle Bill must think we aren't trying very hard to please him," said Kathie, as she stood pulling wisps of straw out of her hair. "He doesn't know how much time we are spending to find the precious picture of his mother."

"Haven't we hunted for it high and low?" Reed asked. "Haven't we pulled up the hay and pushed it and dug into it? Haven't we got our hands and arms full of thistles trying to find it?"

Kathie knew all those things were true. "But maybe by trying a little longer we may find it," she said. " 'If at first you don't succeed, try, try again.' " She was repeating an old saying she had heard Mother say many times.

So that afternoon and the next they spent much time hunting for the precious wallet.

Aunt Jane said she hoped they would find it, for she would like her brother to get back the picture he wanted so much.

Friday afternoon, Kathie said, "I think we ought to have some help. Maybe Linda would come and help us again."

"That's a good idea," her brother agreed. "And maybe Jack would come over and help, too. You go to Linda's house and ask her, and I'll ask Jack."

Jack lived only a half-mile up the road. When he answered the telephone and heard what Reed wanted, he said, "I'll be right over." And it wasn't long before he came into the yard on his bicycle.

Reed was waiting for him. "What's up?"

Jack asked. "How did you happen to lose a wallet in the barn?"

"I didn't lose it. My uncle lost it; and there's something important in it." He told what was in it and how badly it was needed.

"Kathie and I hunted for it a lot of hours. Maybe you'll think of some new place to look. We have only till tomorrow—at two o'clock."

"What will happen if you don't find it?"

"The owner will come and take the horse back to his own place, thirty miles away. Kathie will be heartbroken. Her heart is set on that horse."

Jack parked his bicycle on the back porch beside Reed's. "I'll go to the barn and help you find it," he said.

Meanwhile, Kathie and Linda were coming up the Far Lane. When they had all gathered on the barn floor, Reed said, "Let's talk things over. Let's plan where each of us will go to do our part of the search."

"That's a good idea," Jack agreed. "Then we won't skip any place and we won't get in each other's way."

Jack was a slim lad. He was a little younger than Reed, but he could climb to high places and squeeze through small openings.

"I'll climb up to that corner where the owl is," he offered.

"That's a good idea," Reed said. "I don't

think the wallet would be so high up, but there's no knowing."

"It's so dark in that corner that the wallet wouldn't easily be discovered," said Linda.

"I'll find it if it's there," Jack declared, as he started up the ladder.

Kathie and Linda said they wanted to be together. They took the two scaffolds and the straw mow.

Reed said, "I'll do the basement. If someone has been here and found it, he may have taken out the money and left the wallet down there. The picture might still be in it. It's such a large place down there and so dark that it may take a long time to search everywhere, so the rest of you might come down and help when you've finished your share."

If ever a building was carefully searched for a lost article, it was the old barn that day. Linda remarked that they had searched it with a fine-tooth comb.

Jack had even asked the owl if he knew where the wallet was and the bird had answered with a quick peck at his face, which startled him so that he nearly fell off the beam.

When they were all together again, Reed said to Jack, "Let's you and me go into the passageway that leads to the old shed."

"All right."

The passage began in one corner of the middle part of the big basement. They had to go down some steps at first.

"Gee, it's dark in here!" Jack exclaimed. "And cobwebs are getting in my hair."

The men who did the chores used to go through it in winter to reach the shed, where some of the cows were kept, but it had not been used for a long time.

"Ouch!" Jack exclaimed, as a small creature brushed against his legs in running past.

"That's Snooky chasing a mouse, probably," said Reed.

They went on, slowly, feeling on the brick floor and putting their fingers into crevices in the walls. "We ought to have brought a flashlight," said Reed.

While they were going through the passageway, the girls were sitting on the bench eating apples and talking.

"Why do you want that horse so much?" Linda asked. "I'd much rather ride in an auto than on a horse's back."

"Maybe because I've ridden in autos ever since I can remember; and I never rode a horse till last summer. Maybe because a horse is alive."

"That might be," Linda agreed.

After a while the boys came back. Jack said,

"We've looked in all the nooks and corners; and nary a thing that looks like a wallet have we found."

"And *we* looked in all the cracks and crevices and never a thing that looks like a wallet have *we* found," said Linda.

They were sitting there talking of many things, the four of them, when all at once they heard footsteps coming up the stairs.

They stopped talking and sat listening with all their ears. The stairs creaked under the weight of someone treading on them. There was no mistake about it this time.

In a moment a man the two visitors had never seen came into view from the landing.

"Mr. Plunkett!" Reed greeted him.

The girls jumped to their feet. "Why are you here today?" Kathie demanded. "You were not to come till tomorrow."

"Good afternoon!" he said, in as pleasant a voice as he could manage, which wasn't very pleasant. "I've changed my mind about the horse. I'm not going to sell him."

"Not going to sell him to us?" Reed asked in alarm.

"That's what I said."

"But you promised," Kathie said. "You said you would sell Tom to us for two hundred dollars."

"A person has a right to change his mind,

hasn't he? And it's pretty certain that you children couldn't raise the two hundred dollars. Maybe if you had it right in your hands now, I might take it and leave the horse, but I have to go back home and I'm going to take him with me."

"We might get the money soon," said Kathie.

"If we had more time we might," Reed declared.

"I can't wait. I've been thinking things over. That horse is valuable to me. He knows the milk route. He will stop at the right houses and turn the right corners. I've decided that I'd better not give him up."

Kathie thought of the welt on Tom's back. "Please, Mr. Plunkett, please leave him here. We'll have the money pretty soon and we'll send it to you. He is such a nice gentle horse for us to ride. Please."

But the man was already starting down the narrow stairs to Tom's stall.

Kathie broke into tears. Linda tried to comfort her. "When your father comes home, he will buy another horse for you, I'm sure."

"I don't want another one. This is the horse I want. He is always gentle. He gives us nice rides. We know him and he knows us."

She pulled out her handkerchief and wiped away her tears. Reed said, "Let's go down and see what happens."

All four of them hurried out the big front door and around the corner of the barn. There outside the stable door stood Tom. The man was putting a halter on him.

Tom pulled away and started over to the children. The man yanked the halter. Then he climbed on Tom's back and went off toward the Far Lane.

"I'll never see Tom again," Kathie said, in a broken voice.

They stood there and watched till horse and man disappeared at the end of the lane.

XI

SHAPE
IN THE FOG

A WEEK passed. Every morning Kathie
thought of Old Tom the first thing when she
woke up. "I hope the man is kind to him,"
she said to herself. "I'd like to be sure that
he is not being ill treated."

She remembered the welts on his back. She
remembered how he didn't want to go away
with Mr. Plunkett.

She said to Reed one day as they were going
to school, "Do you s'pose there is any way we
could find out where Tom is and whether he is
being treated kindly?"

"I don't know. We didn't ask the man where
he lives and maybe he wouldn't have told us if
we had, but we know he is at least thirty miles
away."

Every day, when they came home from

school, they looked in the mail box to get the letter they expected from Father and Mother.

One day there was an air-mail letter from Mother that was heavier than usual. It contained snapshots of Father that showed he was getting well. It contained snapshots of some of the beautiful places Mother had seen.

"There is wonderful scenery in Alaska," she wrote. "The mountains are magnificent and the rivers are grand. You'd love it here. I hope you can come here some time. But I haven't seen anything I like better than my own home and you two standing on the porch to greet me."

Then followed a bit of news they didn't like so well: "I'm going to stay a week longer than I expected to. I hope you won't mind too much. Father will be able to walk a little by that time. Won't that be grand?"

"It surely will be grand," Reed said.

Aunt Jane said she was glad the matter of buying that horse was settled. "Though I would have helped a little by loaning you some money if the man would have sold him, I don't really want to be responsible for buying a white elephant," she said.

"But we didn't want to buy a white elephant," said Kathie. "All we wanted to buy was a gentle old horse."

Aunt Jane laughed. "We sometimes call a thing a white elephant when we mean something that will be a great bother—something we will wish we hadn't got."

"Oh, I see," Kathie said.   "White elephants must be a bother, I s'pose."

"And no good to anyone," said Aunt Jane.

Kathie telephoned to Linda one day, "Can't you come over on Saturday? I'm lonely with Mother away so long."

"I'd love to," was the reply.   "I'll be there about two o'clock."

What with making a doll's dress together and playing duets on the piano and looking at a television show, the afternoon passed happily. Still there would be ten days before Mother would be home.

Reed felt it less, for he often stayed after school to play basket ball with the other boys.

One day Aunt Jane said after school, "Kathie, if you will go to the old barn and bring up some apples, I'll make an apple dumpling for dinner tonight."

"I'd love to, Aunt Jane."

It was a cold foggy afternoon. Dark came early these days, so she would have to hurry.

"You'd better put on your heavy sweater," said Aunt Jane. "It's chilly outdoors."

Kathie put on her oldest shoes and her heavy sweater, took the apple basket in hand and started down the lane, bareheaded.

"I wish Reed were along," she said to herself. "That big front door of the barn is very hard to open."

She skipped along, swinging the basket back and forth, wishing she were going to find Old Tom in his stall, wishing she could take a ride on his back.

She came to the gate, climbed over it and went along the well-worn path to the brook. The water was higher than it had been in the summer, so some of the little islands were covered with water.

She wanted to stop and put a little chip in the brook and watch it float downstream, but all at once she noticed that it was getting darker and the fog was thicker. Quickly she hurried on to the barn and filled her basket half full of the big red apples.

A flock of swallows flew in through one of the little windows high up in the end of the barn. She heard a squeak somewhere up in the straw.

"That's a rat," she decided. "Guess I'll hurry out of here."

After she crossed the little brook she glanced back toward the windmill.

In the thick fog and the darkness, she couldn't see things plainly. Then, all at once, she saw something moving in the fog, something that had a familiar shape.

"Could it be? Oh, could it be?" she said aloud, in an excited tone. "It looks like—"

She crossed back over the little bridge and looked hard at something that looked like the tail of a white horse.

"Could it be Tom?" she whispered.

At that moment there came a whinny from the direction of the barn.

"It is Tom!" she shouted. "He is letting me know that he has come back."

Putting the basket of apples down, she ran across the meadow to the door of the stable. There he stood, nosing in the manger for hay.

"Tom! Tom! You came back to us—all alone!" she exclaimed.

She went to his head and patted his neck and smoothed his mane. Then she noticed a new welt on his back. "Has that bad man been whipping you again?" she asked.

She heard someone walking on the barn floor upstairs. Soon a voice that she knew very well called out, "Kathie! Kathie! Where are you?"

"Here, Reed, in the stable. Come down here and see who has come back."

Reed hurried down the little stairs, calling out to her, "Why did you stay down here so long, Kathie? Aunt Jane is anxious about you. You shouldn't give her so much worry."

In a moment he knew. He saw.

"Snakes and bumblebees!" he exclaimed.

"Just look, Reed. Tom has come back to us!" Kathie said in great excitement.

"I'll be jiggered! I'll be double jiggered!" he shouted. "Tom likes us enough to come back thirty miles!"

At the sound of Reed's voice, Tom turned his head and looked in that direction, as much as to say, "Did you think I'd stay away from a place where I'm treated so well! Not as long as I have four good legs to walk with."

"I'll go up in the haymow and pitch some hay down for him. He must be hungry," Reed said.

It was so dark that he could hardly see to find the pitchfork, but finally he found it and put plenty of good hay down into the rack in front of Tom.

"And now you and I had better go to the house," said Reed, when he came back down to the stable.

They went out through the stable door, picked up the basket of apples and were soon at the head of the lane.

XII

TOM IS HAPPY

IN THE next few days Reed and Kathie took many horseback rides in the Barn Meadow and up and down the two lanes.

"Tom enjoys it as much as we do," said Reed one sunny day in November, when they were riding down the Far Lane.

"I think so," Kathie agreed. "He arches his neck as if he was happy to be back again."

"I guess he knows that we'll never strike him with a whip. And we always see that he has plenty of food and water," Reed said.

"Won't Mother and Father be surprised when they come home and see how well we can ride?" said Kathie.

"Probably we won't have Tom that long," Reed reminded her.

"Mother will be home in two weeks," said Kathie. "She'll surely buy him for us."

But that evening the telephone rang. Aunt Jane answered it.

"Yes, a boy of that name lives here," they heard her say. "Yes, I'll call him."

She turned to Reed, saying, "The man on the phone wants to speak to you."

Over the wire Reed heard the voice of a man who seemed to be very angry.

"Has my horse gone back to your place?" he asked. "My name is Plunkett. You must remember me."

"Surely I remember you, Mr. Plunkett," Reed assured him.

"Well, answer me. Has that horse turned up at your place? He's gone off somewhere again."

"Yes, he came back last Thursday."

"Is he there now? Have you kept him in your stable?"

"We haven't kept him, but the stable door is always open and he comes and goes whenever he likes."

Kathie was listening intently. She had guessed who was at the other end of the wire.

"Tell him we want to buy Tom," she said to Reed. "Ask him to wait till Mother comes back."

"Why didn't you let me know?" Mr. Plunkett demanded.

"We couldn't let you know. You didn't tell us where you lived."

"I'm telling you now that I want that horse back. Listen, Sonny. Keep him locked in the stable till I get there. I'll be there the day after tomorrow."

"Oh, Mr. Plunkett, Kathie will be so unhappy."

"I remember her, a pretty girl, but I'm going to show that horse who's boss. If I'm to deliver milk, I must have a horse that will not be running off all the time."

There was a click in the telephone. Reed thought the man had rung off, but in a moment he was speaking again: "I'll be at your place at half-past three, day after tomorrow. If you have two hundred dollars ready to pay for him, you may keep the horse; but if you can't pay for him then, I'll start back home with him quick."

"But, Mr. Plunkett, our father and mother are in Alaska, so Kathie and I can't have so much by that time. Mother will be home in two weeks. If you'll only wait, I'm pretty sure she'll manage it."

"No, I won't wait. I'll bring the horse back. Half-past three, day after tomorrow. Good-by!"

The telephone clicked. He had rung off.

"What did he say?" Kathie asked.

Reed told her. Kathie burst into tears.

Late that evening the telephone rang again. "Alaska calling," the operator said. It was Mother.

Aunt Jane was the only one still up. She had hastened to the telephone.

"We have talked over the matter of buying that horse," Mother said. "We think it would be a good thing for Reed and Kathie to have a gentle faithful old horse. If there is another chance to buy it, will you please help them with the money? We'll repay you when we come home."

"Yes, I'll be glad to. I'm not sure that I have enough here with me, but I'll do what I can."

Something happened to the line just then, so they were cut off.

The next morning she told Kathie and Reed, "I'll help you with buying the horse, but I can't manage all the money. I have only a hundred dollars here. Since your father and mother are willing that you should have him, I'll loan you that, but I can't do any more."

That day passed. Then came the morning of the last day they would have Tom—perhaps.

"Because it's the last day Tom will be here, I'm going down to the barn with you," Kathie said, when Reed started to the barn to feed and water the horse.

It was a lovely sunshiny morning. As they went down the lane, they saw a flock of wild geese flying south, high in the sky. They heard an airplane flying far over their heads.

"Do you s'pose Mr. Plunkett will really come this afternoon and take Tom away?" Kathie asked, as they neared the gate.

"I s'pose he will. And there's no use in our trying any more to find that wallet."

Reed turned on the windmill and the water was soon filling the watering trough. Kathie went into the basement and stood near Tom's stall. Reed went up on the haymow to pitch hay down into Tom's rack.

"Good morning, Tom," Kathie said in her kindest tone.

Tom turned his head as if glad to hear her voice.

"We're going to keep you if we possibly can, Tom," she told him.

When Reed had pitched some hay down into the rack in front of Tom, the horse put his head up and pulled a bunch of it through the spindles that made the rack. He pulled several bunches through, one after another.

After a while a bunch of hay that he tried to pull through wouldn't come down. Kathie watched Tom tug at it with his big teeth. He pulled it and twisted it, pulled it and twisted it. He seemed bound to get that bunch of hay down.

Suddenly Kathie saw something rather large slide down between the spindles and fall into the manger. "I wonder what that was," she said to herself.

She stepped forward and picked it up.

It was dark brown and very smooth!

Reed heard her shout, "I've found it! Tom found it! Here's the wallet!"

"What have you found?" he called down, not able to believe his ears.

"Uncle Bill's wallet. Here it is!"

Reed rushed down the stairs two steps at a time.

"Are you *sure,* Kathie?"

She held it out to him. "Tom pulled it through his rack with some of the hay you pitched down."

Reed stood amazed. "*I* know what happened," he said. "Every time we hunted for the wallet in the hay, we must have pushed it farther down. When I pitched the hay just now, the wallet came along with it. Jeepers! That's lucky!"

"Open it," said Kathie. "Let's see what's in it."

Reed opened the leather wallet. "Here's the picture Uncle Bill wants." He held up a small picture of a lady with a sweet face and lovely eyes.

"No wonder Uncle Bill doesn't want to lose it," he said.

"She looks a good deal like our mother," Kathie said.

"She was our grandmother, you know," Reed told her.

"Why, of course; but I hadn't thought of it."

"Let's see how much money is in the wallet," Kathie said.

Reed opened another part of it and found several ten-dollar bills. Kathie could hardly wait for him to take them out.

"As I hand them to you, we'll count them," he said. He began to take them out, one by one, and hand them to Kathie.

"One, two, three, four, five," she counted. "Fifty dollars!"

"Here are some more, in another compart-

ment." He handed them to her. "One, two, three," she counted aloud. "That makes eighty dollars altogether."

"With Aunt Jane's hundred, we have almost enough," she added.

"We need twenty more. I have at least five dollars in my bank, so we need only fifteen more," Reed said.

In a moment they heard the horn. "Aunt Jane is calling us to come back and get ready for school," Kathie said.

Reed put the bills back in the wallet and they started up to the house.

When they told Aunt Jane, she said she would keep the money for them during the day. It was a long day for Kathie, who was so excited that she could hardly put her mind on her lessons.

When at last school was over she and Reed hurried home and went directly down to the barn.

"I'll come in a little while," Aunt Jane said. "I would like to see Old Tom once more before the man takes him away."

Reed stuffed the money down to the very bottom of his pocket.

He and Kathie hadn't been at the barn very long before they heard Linda calling from the big front door. They were still down in the stable patting Old Tom and talking about how

they could possibly get the rest of the money
for him.

"Come on down," Kathie called up to her.

"See what I found just inside the big front
door," she said, as she handed something to
Reed. "A little stone had been placed on it to
keep it from blowing away."

It was a piece of white paper folded twice.
"I'll be tripple jiggered!" he exclaimed.
"Listen to this: 'I am the chap who has been
sleeping in your barn. One rainy morning I
thought you would catch me when I slept late
and Reed came downstairs. I have been down
on my luck and didn't have any money, so I
was surely glad to find this old barn with plenty
of good hay to sleep on. A few times I took
one of the apples for breakfast. Now I have a
good job. I want to give you something for all
this, so here is a ten-dollar bill. Please accept
it with my thanks. J. T. R.' "

"What wonderful luck!" said Kathie. "Now
we have almost enough to buy Tom when Mr.
Plunkett comes."

Linda had been trying to tell them something,
but in the excitement of the letter she hadn't
found a chance. Now she held out an envelope.
"Father sent this to you for letting him take
Tom for the ploughing," she said.

When Reed opened it, he found a five-dollar
bill. "I'll be jiggered again!" Reed exclaimed,

holding it up for Kathie to see.

"That makes just the hundred we need," she said.

"With what Aunt Jane has promised," said Reed. "I wonder why she doesn't come."

Just then they heard her voice. "Where are you?"

Kathie started to go up and bring her down. "We'll all go up," said Reed.

Tom turned toward the door and went out into the meadow. Reed and the girls went up to the big barn floor, where Aunt Jane was standing looking up at the roof, listening to the doves.

Reed opened the big doors wide. The sunlight streamed in.

They all went out of the barn and were going down the incline when they heard a man's voice saying, "Come here, Tom. I've come to take you back. I'll teach you to run off!"

They all hurried around the corner of the barn. Mr. Plunkett was trying to put a halter on Tom's neck.

"I've come to take the horse," he said. "The time is up."

"But we have the money ready," Reed told him.

"I've changed my mind. I'm going to take him back."

He was about to mount Tom when Aunt Jane

spoke up, "You can't do that," she said, in a determined tone of voice. "You can't go back on your word to these children. Reed and Kathie have the money; you must keep your part of the bargain."

She took a hundred dollars out of her hand bag and handed it to Reed.

"You can see that the children have kept their part of the bargain," she said. "You ought to be ashamed not to keep yours."

Mr. Plunkett was so astonished that he could hardly speak; but slowly he took the halter off Tom's neck.

"I s'pose you're right," he admitted. "I'll keep my word. But I want my money—and quick."

He came over and Reed handed him the roll of bills. Mr. Plunkett took his time to count them.

"Correct," he said. "Good day!"

He walked off toward the road.

"Thank you, dear Aunt Jane," said Kathie. "Thank you a lot."

"You certainly helped," said Reed.

"I'd like to see you ride the horse," said Aunt Jane.

Reed ran to the barn for the bridle and put it on Tom. He stepped up on the stump and mounted the horse.

"Have a ride?" he asked Kathie.

"I'd love to."

She stepped up on the stump. Reed helped her up; and Tom started off across the Barn Meadow.

It was a pretty sight—Tom with his neck arched proudly, Reed holding the bridle rein so well and Kathie sitting up straight and not holding on to anything.

THE END